My River 나의 강 ● 이원로 시선집

Lee Won-Ro's 11th Anthology
이원로 11번째 시선집

My River 나의 강

차례

제1부
다리

Part 2

Our Home

제2부

우리 집

Part 3

The Tomorrow Within Today

제3부

오늘 안의 내일

Part 4

The Tunnel of Waves

제4부
파도의 터널

Part 5

The Teacup and the Sea

제5부
찻잔과 바다

My River 나의 강

Prologue

My River

A song of love that
Comes down from high
Enters deep into my heart
And becomes my river.
I don't know why
It happens this way,
But the wave of love
Never stops, and
The river of joy always flows
In the depth of my heart.

A voice of consolation
Resounding from the depths
Turns into my song
Shaking the soul soundly.
Why things are done this way
I have no way to find out,
But the tunes of solace are
Incessant evermore, and
In the depth of my soul
Ripples the river of healing.

(From "A Flute Player")

프롤로그

나의 강

높은 곳에서 내려오는
사랑의 노래
가슴에 깊이 들어와
나의 강이 되지
왜 그렇게 되는지
나는 잘 모르지만
그 사랑의 물결은
언제나 그침이 없고
나의 가슴 깊은 곳에는
늘 기쁨의 강이 흐르지

깊은 곳에서 울려오는
위로의 목소리
심령을 깊이 흔드는
나의 노래가 되지
왜 이렇게 되는지
나는 알 길이 없지만
위로의 음률은
언제나 그치지 않고
나의 심령 깊은 속에는
늘 치유의 강이 물결치지

("피리 부는 사람" 중에서)

제1부

Bridge
다리

Water

Does water make a way?

That's what it looks like.

But in fact,

Along the original path

The water is flowing.

Does water know its way?

That's what it's supposed to be.

But in reality,

A gravity wave draws water

To form a river.

물

물이 길을 내어 가는가
그렇게도 보여지리
그러나 실은
본래 있는 길을 따라
물이 흐르지

물은 본래 길을 아는가
그렇게도 여겨지지
그러나 실은
중력파가 물을 끌어
강을 이루어가지

Bridge-1

To tie up mind to mind,

To link thought to thought.

To combine the soul with the soul,

You and I will put the bridge.

To make us reach the heavens.

Cloud Bridge,

Wind Bridge,

And Fire Bridge

Are amazingly being built

Countless times without knowing.

Life is a history of the Bridge

Bridge of longing

Bridge of joy

Bridge of sorrow.

다리-1

마음에 마음을 맺으려
생각을 생각에 이으려
영혼과 영혼을 합하려
너와 나 다리를 놓아가지

우리를 하늘에 닿게 하려
구름다리
바람다리
불다리를
모르는 사이 무수히
놀랍게 놓아준다

삶은 다리의 역사
동경의 다리
기쁨의 다리
슬픔의 다리

Bridge-2

Following the eager eyeshot,
Within the reach of aspiration,
Countless bridges are laid.

An indomitable longing crosses
The river and the sea,
Into the land of the stars,
And places numerous bridges
Over the end of the universe,
Creating a space network
With circuits and synapses.

Bridge of Light and Darkness
A bridge where dreams intersect
Bridge of grace and peace

다리-2

간절한 눈길을 따라
열망이 닿는 곳으로
무수한 다리가 놓여가지

잠재울 수 없는 갈망이
강을 건너 바다를 넘어
별나라로 우주 끝으로
셀 수 없는 다리를 놓아가지
회로와 시냅스를 이루어
우주 망을 만들어가지

빛과 어둠의 다리
꿈이 교차하는 다리
은혜와 평강의 다리

Bridge-3

Building of a bridge of you and I
Started long before the world was born.
Over the Invisible countless
Bridges of twists and turns,
We have arrived at this pont of time-space.

Towards the attraction,
Following the call signal,
To flourish rich glory,
Let's build our bridge
Irreplaceable to anything,

You and my bridge will
Connect heaven with earth;
The bridge of truth.
It is to bear the fruit of the promise;
The bridge of eternity.

다리-3

너와 나의 다리는
세상이 생기기 오래전
벌써 놓이기 시작했지
보이지 않는 무수한
우여곡절의 다리를 넘어
시공의 한 점 여기에 왔지

끌리는 곳을 향하여
부르는 신호를 따라
풍성한 영광을 피어갈
무엇과도 바꿀 수 없는
우리의 다리를 세워가지

너와 나의 다리는
하늘과 땅을 이어줄
진실의 다리이지
약속의 열매를 맺을
끝없이 뻗어나갈
무궁의 다리이지

Freedom

With all their heart and soul,

The fingers

Tapping on the keyboard are

Going deeper and deeper.

With all their body and mind,

The hearts

Playing the flute are

Being lifted up higher and higher.

As much as they have been caught

They'll be free.

When they're completely immersed,

They'll be most free.

자유

심혈을 기울여
건반을 두드리는
손가락들
깊이 더 깊이 빠져들어 간다

몸과 마음 다해
피리를 부는
가슴들
높이 더 높이 들려 올라간다

잡힌 만큼
자유로워지지
완전히 잠겨질 때
가장 자유롭게 되리

That Sound

Can you hear that?
We know who they are.
We know why.
Begging for an answer
They make sounds.

An incredible encounter of fate is
Spreading out at the estuary.

Blowing wind
Whooper swans that pass by
A swirling wave
The hesitating sun
Each makes its unique sound
From their ardent desires.

Who knows how long they'll be together?
Who knows how far they're going together?

Can you hear that?
We know what they want.
We know who they're waiting for.
The reverberation of this stage
Casts a glimpse beyond.

저 소리

저 소리 들리나
누구인지 알지
왜 그러는지 알리
대답을 간구하며
소리를 내리

놀라운 운명의 만남이
강어귀에 펼쳐진다

불어오는 바람
스쳐 가는 큰고니들
넘실거리는 물결
머무적거리는 해
저마다 깊이 간직된
간절한 소리를 내리

언제까지 함께 할지 누가 알랴
어디까지 같이 갈지 누가 알랴

저 소리 들리나
무얼 바라는지 알지
누굴 기다리는지 알지
이 무대의 울림이
너머를 흘끗 보여 준다

The Sound of Wind in Eulalia Field

Dr. Kim is a passionate climber,
He sent me the sound of the wind
In the field of eulalia
On Mount Cheonseong in a video.

The strong winds are dancing
With a group of silver grass in all their might.
Their head, limbs and torso are shaking wildly.
I don't know if it's a hard dance or a dance of joy.
The heart and mind of the beholder will measure.

The sound of the wind echoes the whole mountain
And touch the sky beyond overflowing clouds.
It crosses the hills and the fields to reach the sea.

Where does it come? Where does it go?
It may pass through here not to rein but for friendship.
Showing the free flow and the wholehearted dance,
It may try to infuse deeply into the soul
A life of no hesitation and open mind.

That's it!
It must be the sound of the joys of freedom!
It is trying to get everyone to know that.
I'm sure he was dragged there by the sound.

억새밭 바람 소리

김 박사는 열정적 등산객
천성산 억새밭 바람 소리를
동영상에 담아서 내게 보냈다

세차게 불어오는 바람이
억새 무리와 혼신의 춤을 춘다
머리 사지 몸통이 마구 흔들린다
버거운 춤인지 환희의 무도인지
보는 이의 머리와 가슴이 가늠하리

기이한 바람 소리는 온 산을 울리고
흐르는 구름 떼를 넘어 하늘에 이른다
구릉과 벌판을 건너 바다에 닿는다

어디서 보내 어디로 가는 바람인지
군림이 아니라 사귀러 여길 지나가리
흐름의 자유와 억새의 혼신무도를 보여
주저 없는 마음 거리낌 없는 삶을
영혼에 깊이 불어넣어 주려서리

바로 그거야! 그걸 모두에 알리려 서지
분명 자유를 구가하는 바람 소리야!
그 소리에 끌려 그가 거길 다녀왔으리

Door

What's worthless in the world is

Not a single.

To tell you something different,

Each is waiting for you and

Calling you to get in there.

It's an open door.

If you pass by casually,

Nothing.

If you tilt your mind,

Wonderful world.

You and I pass by many noble gates

Without knowing anything.

문

세상에 쓸모없는 건
하나도 없지
각기 다른 걸 알려주려고
너를 기다리고 있는
거기로 들어가게 부르는
열린 문이지

무심히 스쳐 가면
아무것도 아니지
유심히 마음을 기울이면
불가사의 세상이지
수많은 고귀한 문을 너와 나
무언지도 모르고 지나가지

Circuit

Across the mountains beyond the sea
There is the land of eternity
Where the dreams of you and me live.

How beautiful the meeting
Between you and me was!
How sublime the love
Of you and me is!
How inscrutable the farewell
Between you and me will be!

Across the constellation beyond the galaxy
There is the world of endless time.
Yearnings of you and me live there.

How beautiful are the flowers
In blooming and fading.
How noble are the stars
On their way home.
How wondrous is the circuit
Predestined for you and me.

회로回路

산 너머 바다 건너
거기는 영원의 나라
너와 나의 꿈이 사는 곳

얼마나 아름다웠나
너와 나의 만남
얼마나 숭고한가
너와 나의 사랑
얼마나 경이로울까
너와 나의 이별

성좌 너머 은하 건너
거기는 무궁의 시간
너와 나의 동경이 살지

얼마나 아름다운가
피고 지는 꽃들
얼마나 숭고한가
별들의 가는 길
얼마나 경이로운가
너와 나의 예정 회로

A Pledge

What pledge is this ship making?
In a crowded harbor,
They raise their sails
And blow their trumpets.

'We'll be back full!'
The cry of resolution is high.
They don't know what's going to happen,
Who they are going to bump into.
In an uncertain sea
They are full of expectations.
As much as the wings fly,
As much as they promise
Are they going to catch it?

What you make a promise to
Is great, but
Why you make a pledge is
More valuable.

다짐

무슨 다짐을 다지며
출항하는 배인가
북적거리는 항구에서
돛을 올리고 나팔을 분다

가득 싣고 돌아오리라
다짐의 외침 드높다
무슨 일이 일어날지
누구와 부닥칠지
불확정의 바다에서
기대의 눈빛 가득하다
날개 치는 만큼
다짐하는 만큼
잡게 되려는가

무얼 다짐하는지도
장하나
왜 다짐을 하는지가
더욱 값지지

Streaks of Rain

In the middle of the night
Between the vigilant streetlights
There's something faintly flickering.
When I opened the window and looked closely,
Streaks of rain are blowing in the wind.

The streets are swept by the wind and rain.
Street trees waiting in line are
Sweating out and being baptized.
Beyond the clouds above the rain,
The stars will dance and twinkle.

Because it shows something
Even in the deep darkness.
It's not an endless void.
Because It rains to sprout,
It's not a deserted world.

빗발

한밤중을 지키는
가로등 사이에서
희미하게 무언가 어른댄다
창을 열고 자세히 보니
바람에 날리는 빗발이다

거리는 비바람에 휲이고
줄 서 기다리는 가로수들
진땀 빼며 세례를 받는다
빗발 위 구름 너머에서는
별들이 반짝이며 춤추겠지

짙은 어둠 속에서도
무언 갈 보여주니
끝없는 공허는 아니리
싹 틔울 비를 내리니
버려진 세상은 아니리

The Others

A shining sky blooms

From her smiling face.

Her eyes won't budge anymore.

I'm sure she got a message

From over there.

She held it firmly and kept it

Deep in her heart, not missing it.

The one who catches the amazing future

Would live in eternal joy,

And the others can't be seen anymore.

딴것

미소 짓는 그녀의 얼굴에서
빛나는 하늘이 피어나온다
그녀의 눈빛도 더는 흔들리지 않는다

분명 그녀는 너머에서 보내온
메시지를 받았으리
그걸 그녀는 놓치지 않고 굳게 붙들어
가슴 깊이 간직하였으리

놀라운 미래를 잡은 이
영원한 기쁨 안에 살리
딴것은 이제 안 보이리

The Gaze of Time

Your days of sweating hard and dragging,

Without anyone knowing,

Have changed dramatically;

Nobody knows

Whether this was

Due to cultivation

By someone watering you

Or by the increase of your annual rings.

Now is the time

When you're willing to follow and hum.

You did what you were told to do,

Or did you do it by yourself?

The gaze of time is

Smiling and passing by.

시간의 눈빛

버겁게 땀 흘리며
끌고 가던 나날이
어느 사이

누가 물을 주어
가꾸었는지
나이테가 늘어나며
달라졌는지

모르는 사이
기꺼이 따라가며
홍얼대는 시간이 되지

시킨 걸 한 건가
혼자 해 냈나
씩 웃고 스쳐 가는
시간의 눈빛

A Recess

Winter branches are frozen.
Winter hearts look languid and haggard.
Did all the energy evaporate?
Have their ideas hit the bottom?

They're worn out on the outside,
But not on the inside.
A recess is the time of concentration.
It's the birthplace of transformation.
An amazing rebound is
Showing off its posture there.

Rest is a bridge that passes
Through here and goes to the next.
It's emptying today
To contain tomorrow.

휴게休憩

겨울 가지들이 얼어붙어 있다
겨울 마음들이 나른하고 까칠하다
에너지가 모두 증발했나
아이디어가 바닥을 쳤나

고갈된 모습이나
그 안은 안 그러리
휴게는 결집의 시간
전환의 발상지이지
놀라운 리바운드가
거기서 자세를 뽐내리

휴게는 여기를 지나
다음으로 가는 다리
내일을 담으려
오늘을 비우고 있다

Brain and Heart

The wind is rushing.

The clouds are threatening.

Do the leaves that are still hanging

Ask only for a goodwill?

Clouds are rising in the sky.

On a path in the woods,

Raindrops are falling.

The fallen leaves are flying.

The brain says

'That's right!'

But my heart goes, 'It's not yet'

With a bitter smile.

머리와 가슴

바람이 재촉한다
구름이 으름장을 놓는다
아직 달려 있는 잎들은
선처만 바라고 있나

하늘엔 구름이 일고
숲속 오솔길에
빗방울이 떨어진다
가랑잎이 날린다

머리는 '그렇지!'
끄덕이는데
가슴은 '아직 아닌데!'
쓴웃음 짓지

Surfing

We surf through

Space on time.

With the stars, you and I glide

Through time and space.

Thoughts stick out their tentacles.

The heart spreads its wings.

We are carried in the clouds by the wind,

Flying into the secret kingdom.

Because there is a caller,

We'll be pulled in endlessly.

Longing rises in our hearts

As an amazing meeting awaits.

서핑

우리는 시간을 타고
공간을 서핑한다
별들과 함께 너와 나
시공을 활공하지

생각이 촉수를 내밀고
마음이 날개를 펼치어
바람을 타고 구름에 실려
비밀왕국으로 날아들지

불러들이는 이 있기에
한없이 우리는 끌려들어 가리
놀라운 만남이 기다리니
그리움이 마음에 솟구쳐 오르지

A Bird Call

There is a biting wind in the gray sky.
A dreary fog covers the forest.
There is no shadow on the forest road.
A bird call breaking through the silence
Keeps sending a monotone signal.

He can't stop calling some one.
It's a note of appeal after a protest.
There's a sad tone because of no reply.
He was trying to climb higher,
But he was not able to.
It's because he didn't get what he wanted.

Soon the bird's chirping stops.
Flapping wings hit the air.
He must be on the way to meet the responder.
What and how you begged.
You don't always get what you want.

새소리

회색 하늘에 칼바람이 분다
음산한 안개가 숲을 가려온다
숲길에는 아무 그림자도 없다
적막을 깨고 들려오는 새소리
계속 단음계 신호를 보낸다

누군가를 부르는지 그침이 없다
항의를 지나서 호소의 음조이다
답이 없어 섭섭한 음색도 섞였다
오르려는 데 못 올라 애타서인가
구하는 걸 못 얻어서 그러는 거리

이윽고 새의 지저귐이 멎는다
퍼덕이는 날개가 허공을 친다
응답 듣고 만나러 가는 길이리
무엇을 어떻게 간구하였는지
받을 건 늘 바라는 대로는 아니지

True Taste

'We know the true taste of bread only when we die.'

The words of a wise man who has been through a lot.

He is serious and doesn't seem to joke.

He reiterates the taste of bread is bitter by nature,

But when we live here, it tastes like honey.

In a huff and begging

We fight each other to eat such bitter bread.

We'll find out the true taste of the world

on the last day.

Like this kind of bread,

Life goes by like this.

We live without knowing the true taste of life.

That's how we get it.

That's how we live it.

참맛

'밥의 참맛은 죽을 때나 알지'
산전수전 다 겪은 현자의 말씀이다
우스갯소리 아닌 진지한 얼굴이다
밥맛은 본래 쓴데
여기서 살 때는 꿀맛이란다

우리는 허덕이며 구걸하며
다투어 그런 밥을 먹고 살지
세상의 참맛은
끝 날에야 알아본단다

이렇게 먹는 밥처럼
삶은 이렇게 지나가지
삶의 참맛 모르고 한평생 살지
그렇게 받으니
그렇게 살리

One Spot in the Moment

The smile of the moment
You bloom gives off
The history of the beginning.
The vision of the future unfolds
In the eyes of the moment
You stare.

The performance you give
In an invisible point
Comforts all the sorrows of the world.
The joyful song you sing
In a spot of amazing space-time
Resonates across the universe.

Moments aren't moments.
There's eternity in the moment.
The moment is eternal.
One point is not one point.
In one spot, there's infinitude.
One point is endless.

순간 안에 한 점

당신이 피워내는
순간의 미소 가운데
태초의 내력이 풍겨납니다
당신이 응시하는
순간의 눈빛 속에
미래의 전경이 펼쳐옵니다

보이지도 않는 한 점에서
당신이 울려주는 연주가
세상 모든 슬픔을 위로합니다
놀라운 시공 한 점에서
당신이 불려주는 기쁜 노래가
우주를 넘어 울려 퍼져갑니다

순간은 순간이 아니야
순간 안에 영원이 들어 있어
순간이 영원이지
한 점은 한 점이 아니야
한 점 안에 무궁이 들어 있지
한 점이 무궁이야

They

Though they don't know

Why,

Or for what,

They have to go

Through this life

Along the given path.

In a world full of ups and downs,

They are to meet in their tears

The day of amazing reconciliation.

그들

왜인지
어째서인지
그들은 모르나

주어진 길을 따라
그들은 여기의 삶을
지나가야 하지

파란곡절波瀾曲折의 세상에서
그들은 눈물 가운데
놀라운 화목의 날을 만나리

제2부

Our Home
우리 집

Outside the Window

Life is energy,
Energy is the soul.
As energy is immortal
By way of a relay race,
Life is forever.

Before seeing the shape,
There was life.
The form is for a moment,
But the life is immortal
Outside the window.

Energy enters the visible world
To reveal itself for some time.
After its task is comleted here,
In order of an endless relay race,
It takes a loop line outside the window.

A form is for a while,
But the life is immortal.
A shape is temporary.
But the soul is eternal
Outside the window.

창밖에서

생명은 에너지
에너지는 영혼
끝없는 이어달리기로
에너지가 불멸이니
생명은 영원하지

형상을 보기 전에
생명이 있었지
형체는 잠시이나
생명은 창밖에서
영원무궁하지

에너지가 모습을 드러내
보이는 세상으로 나온다
창안에서 제구실을 다 하면
이어달리기 순서를 따라
창밖에서 환상선環狀線을 타지

형상은 잠깐이나
생명은 영구하지
모습은 순간이나
영혼은 창밖에서
불사불멸하리

Center

At the center of the universe

Who lives?

Surprisingly, you and me.

They and all of them

Live in the center.

Unfathomable

And inevitable

Great power and wisdom

Put body, mind and soul

In the center

When the universe opens with the Big Bang

All were invisible one at the center.

Even if the universe expands endlessly

The center will stay always at the center.

Each one lives as it is in its center.

중심

우주의 중심에는
누가 사는가
놀랍게도 너와 나이지
그들도 다른 이들도 모두
중심에서 살지

헤아릴 수 없는
거역할 수 없는
큰 능력과 지혜가
몸과 마음과 영혼을
중심에 세워주었지

빅뱅으로 우주가 열릴 때
모두는 중심 안 보이는 하나였지
우주가 끝없이 팽창해가도
중심은 언제나 중심으로 머물리
각자는 그 중심에서 그대로 살리

Peace

Time is always

Wiser than us.

We always try in this world

To make peace by quarrel.

Time doesn't hesitate because

There is no real peace here.

Time always beckons us

To the country of peace.

We are sloppy and

Ignore the signals of time.

평화

시간은 늘 우리보다
더 현명하지

우리는 이 세상에서 늘
다투며 평화를 이루려 하지

시간은 머뭇대지 않지
여기엔 진정한 평화가 없기에

시간은 늘 평화의 나라로
우리를 손짓해 부르지

우리는 제멋에 겨워
시간의 신호를 무시하지

Giving and Receiving

Are you worried because
You haven't received it yet?
You're supposed to receive what you receive,
Because Giver
Knows the heart to receive.

You've already received it, or
If you haven't received it yet,
You'll get it soon.
What to give is supposed to give
When Receiver
Knows the heart of Giver.

What you receive is
Supposed to give.
Giving is
Supposed to be received.
Giving is receiving.

주기와 받기

아직 못 받아서
걱정스러운가
받을 것은 받게 되어 있어
주는 이
받는 마음 알기에

이미 받았거나
아직 못 받았으면
곧 받게 될 거야
줄 것은 주게 되어 있어
받는 이
주는 마음 알게 될 때

받는 것은
주게 되어 있어
주는 것은
받게 되어 있어
주는 것이 받는 것이지

Late Autumn Leaves

Under the cold windy sky
under a naked tree
Late autumn leaves are stunningly brilliant.

It seems to be not wrong to say
That there is a time for everyone.
In the shade of big trees,
They were pushed without light.

Life is not fair.
So I thought it was over.
But late-blooming flames
Appear to decorate their exit.

The grand finale is near.
Their hearts will become more earnest.
They'll pour out amazing colors.

늦단풍

찬 바람 부는 하늘 아래
알몸이 된 나무 밑에
늦단풍이 놀랍게 눈부시다

누구나 한때가 있다더니
틀린 말은 아닌 듯싶다
큰 나무들의 그늘에 가려
빛도 없이 밀려 살았지

삶은 공평치 않아
이미 끝난 줄로 알았더니
늦게 피어나는 불꽃으로
퇴장을 장식해 주려나보다

대단원이 가까워졌다
더욱 간절한 마음이 되리
놀라운 빛깔을 쏟아내리

The Bell Is Ringing

The bell is ringing.
Pigeons fly up.
The flags flutter.
The trumpet sound resonates.
The ceremony will begin.

They must be drawn together by
The emotion they had never felt
And by the great force
They could not resist.
Their waiting eyes and longing smiles
Will bloom into a shining future.

The sky is dazzling.
The sea is peaceful.
The bell is ringing.
The trumpet sound resonates.
The march will begin.

Your pleading eyes!
Let's wish them happiness!
Let's celebrate
A meeting of chastity,
Perfect union,
Amazing completion.

종이 울린다

종이 울린다
비둘기가 날아오른다
깃발이 나부낀다
나팔 소리가 울려 퍼진다
예식이 시작되리

느껴본 적 없는 감동과
거역할 수 없는 큰 힘에 끌려
그들은 함께 되었으리
기다리는 그들의 눈빛과
바라보는 미소는
빛나는 미래를 피워내리

하늘이 눈부시다
바다는 평화롭다
종이 울린다
나팔 소리가 울려 퍼진다
행진이 시작되리

탄원하는 눈들아
행복을 빌자
축하하자
순결의 만남을
완전한 결합을
놀라운 완성을

Shade

Everyone was born in the shade.

We live in the shade

And go back in the shade.

Who do you live under today?

What shade shall I stay in tomorrow?

How long do we live in

The shadow of arrogance?

How many shades of idols

Tame our lives.

Until we enter the shadow of rest.

The light is so intense that

We can't even figure out the outline.

We will never understand the eternity,

But only live in that shade.

그늘

누구나 그늘에서 태어나
그늘 안에서 살다가
그늘 안으로 돌아가지
너는 오늘 누구 그늘에서 살아가나
나는 내일 어떤 그늘에 머무를까

얼마나 긴 세월을 우리는
오만의 그늘에서 사는가
얼마나 많은 우상의 그늘이
우리의 삶을 길들여가나
안식의 그늘에 들 때까지

빛살이 너무나 강렬하니
어찌 윤곽이나 헤아리랴
영원무궁은 파악 못 하리
오직 그 그늘에서 살아가지

Dance of Life

The eyes of clever wisdom
Snatched the deeply cherished,
Invisible dance of life.

It's an indescribable rhythmic gymnastics
That duplicates and transcribes genes.
It's a whole body dance that transmits life.

The beads vibrate and the strings get tangled.
Countless dances that are hung up and curl up
Are creating life.

In the cells of your and my body,
Life dances, panting and
Fluttering to pass on life.

생명의 춤

영악한 지혜의 눈들이
깊이 간직된 안 보이는
생명의 춤을 낚아챘다

유전자를 복제하고 전사하는
형언할 수 없이 놀라운 율동체조
생명을 전수하는 혼신의 춤이다

구슬이 진동하고 끈이 얽힌다
끊고 잇고 웅크렸다 뻗어내는
무수한 춤이 생명을 지어간다

너와 나의 몸 세포 안에서
생명이 생명을 전수하려
설레며 헐떡이며 춤춘다

Escape

'Discretion is the better part of valor"

These are the words of a wise old man.

Even when you can't win and see the next,

You shouldn't rush to score an own goal.

Is our path a journey of escape?

We're running away to be free.

We miss peace and run away.

We run away to plan the next.

We run away from the dark to find the light.

Are fugitives so revolutionaries?

Because we want to live and

don't want to be trapped,

In search of refuge

We always run away.

도망

'삼십육계 중 줄행랑이 제일이란다'
예부터 내려오는 현자의 말씀이다
이길 수 없으니 다음이 안 보인다고
자살골을 넣으려 돌진해서야 되겠나

우리의 길은 도망의 여정인가
자유롭게 되려 도망가는 거지
평화가 그리워서 도망하지
다음을 도모하려 도망가지
빛을 찾아 어둠에서 도망치리
도망자는 그러니 혁명가인가

살고 싶기에
갇히기 싫어
피난처를 찾아
우리는 늘 도망치지

Vitality

Vitality is rising!

I can't see but I can feel it.

I can't hear it, but it resounds.

It's a sign of tomorrow.

Of course, the buds that grow out,

Even in the faded and the withered,

In the eyes that look deeply,

Amazing vitality is crouching inside.

A gift of promise that has been reserved

To open joy in the midst of sorrow,

To shine a light in the dark,

The vital elements contained in the genes

Are the evidences of a mysterious life.

Being carried on marvelous circuits,

They will grow the generations endlessly.

활력活力

활력이 피어오른다
안 보이지만 느껴지지
안 들리나 울려 퍼지지
내일을 알려주는 징후이다

돋아나는 꽃봉오리야 물론
바랜 것들 시든 것들 안에도
깊이 들여다보는 눈에는
놀라운 활력이 웅크리고 있지
슬픔 가운데서 기쁨을 열어줄
어둠 가운데서 빛을 비춰줄
예비 된 약속의 선물이지

유전자에 담긴 활력소들은
오묘한 생명의 증거들이지
불가사의한 회로에 실려 가며
끝없이 세대를 키워가리

Two Magpies

Along the snowy forest road
The sound of magpies is loud.
There's a high octave that screams
With a reluctant short reply.

Since snow is piled up and there is nothing to eat,
One insists on going to the forest across the river;
Another hesitates about whether it will be a good move.
It's a dispute between insistence and hesitation;
It's a quarrel of conviction that
Only there is the way to live and
Doubts about what to do if it's worse?

There must be someone who missed his way to live
Because he turned around in doubts.
Someone has fallen into the path of downfall
Because he was so overconfident.

두 마리 까치

눈 오는 숲길을 따라
까치 소리가 요란하다
호들갑 떠는 높은 옥타브와
마지못해 하는 짧은 대꾸다

눈이 쌓여 먹을게 동나가니
강 건너 숲으로 가자는 주장과
거기라고 별세상일 거냐는
주저의 말다툼이지
오직 거기만이 살길이라는 확신과
더 나쁘면 어쩔까 걱정하는
의심의 논쟁이지

의심이 지나쳐 돌아섰기에
살길을 놓쳐버린 이 있으리
너무나 과신했기에
몰락의 길로 떨어진 이 있으리

The Realm Divided Into Three

You heart and my heart are
The realm divided into three:
A country of doubt,
Kingdom of obedience, and
The realm of treason.
Which kingdom is the strongest?

Depending on our survival strategy
Frequently the territory will change;
Getting bigger and smaller
Disappear and emerge.

Until great wisdom and insight
Rule over division
To realize complete country,
Eternal kingdom and
A world of joy,
The realm divided will always wrestle.

삼분천하

너와 나의 마음은
삼분천하이지
의심의 나라
순종의 왕국
반역의 세상
그중 어느 왕국이 가장 센가

생존전략을 따라
수시로 영역은 변하리
커지고 작아지고
사라지고 생겨나리

완전한 나라
영원한 왕국
기쁨의 세상을 이루려
큰 지혜와 통찰력이
분열을 다스릴 때까지
삼분천하는 늘 씨름하리

Festival

Who says the festival is over?
Even if it rains or snows
The festival will continue.
In the depths, all over the world,
A shout of cheers resounds and
Fireworks are in full swing.
Where there is a meeting
There is always a festival.

The meeting is beginning;
The beginning begins at
The end of the end.
Because the beginning is endless
The festival will never end.

Who says the festival is over?
Because the end is the beginning
The festival is held endlessly.
In the depths of you and me,
In every corner of the universe,
A majestic festival takes place.
Where joy lives,
There will always be a festival.

축제

누가 축제는 끝났다 하나
비가 와도 눈이 내려도
축제는 계속되리
깊은 곳에서 온 세상에서
환호의 외침 들려오리
불꽃놀이가 한창이리
만남이 있는 곳에는
언제나 축제가 있지

만남은 시작
시작은 끝이 끝나는
데서 시작되지
시작이 무궁하기에
축제는 끝이 없으리

누가 축제는 끝났다 하나
끝이 곧 시작이기에
축제는 쉼 없이 열리지
너와 나의 깊은 곳에서
우주의 구석구석에서
장엄한 축제가 벌어진다
기쁨이 사는 곳에서는
언제나 축제가 계속되리

Our Home

Looking down

From the space station,

The whole earth is our home.

When I board the Mars helicopter*,

The whole solar system

Becomes our home.

When we go deep in the Voyager**,

The whole universe

Turns into our home.

The day we enter beyond that,

The kingdom there

Will also become our home.

* Helicopter "Ingenuity" that flew on Mars recently

** "Voyager twin spacecrafts" in deep space exploration past Jupiter and Saturn

우리 집

우주정거장에서
내려다보니
온 지구가 우리 집이네

화성 헬리콥터*에
올라타 보니
온 태양계가 우리 집이 된다

보이저**를 타고
깊이 들어가 보니
온 우주가 우리 집으로 바뀌지

그 너머로 들어서는 날
거기의 온 왕국도 또한
우리 집이 되리

* 최근 화성에서 시험 비행한 헬리콥터 "Ingenuity"
** 목성, 토성을 지나 심우주 탐사 중인 "Voyager 쌍둥이 우주선"

Traffic Light

Whether it missed the traffic light
Or skipped in a hurry,
The spirit of spring is clear in winter.
There is already a fog of spring
In the distant mountains.

The sun is already rushing north
Toward the equator.
The gentry busy with landing on Mars
Are struggling to plan time and space.
Everyone is bustling and pushing and pulling.
The traffic lights are very busy.

The cars that have met on time
Run at full speed, looking only ahead.
The street fluctuates due to the passing force.
I can't take my eyes off the traffic lights and
Wait for my time to come sometime.

신호등

신호등을 잘 못 보았는지
급한 마음에 건너뛰었는지
겨울 속에 봄기운이 완연하다
먼발치 야산에는 벌써
봄 안개가 서려온다

태양은 이미 적도를 향해
북쪽으로 서둘러 달려오고
화성 착륙에 분주한 무리는
시공을 도모하느라 법석이다
모두 부산하고 밀고 밀린다
신호등은 눈코 뜰 새가 없다

제시간을 만난 차들은 온통
앞만 보고 전속력으로 달린다
스쳐 가는 힘에 가로가 들썩댄다
나는 신호등에서 눈을 못 떼고
언젠가 올 내 때를 기다린다

Voice

It's not a sound, it's a voice
Not the sound of the wind
It's someone's voice calling out there.

Can you hear the sea voice?
A voice from a distant mountain
A voice that crosses the horizon
Do you know who it is and why.

Deep in the quiet time,
There will always be the voice,
But it can't be heard and disappear,
Covered by noise and buried in dust.

Your cheers
And my sighs
Will be mixed there.

목소리

소리가 아니라 목소리지
바람 소리가 아니라
거기서 부르는 누군가의 목소리지

바다목소리가 들리나
먼 산이 부르는 목소리
지평을 넘어오는 목소리
누군지 왜인지 아는가

고요한 시간 깊은 데는
언제나 목소리 있을 터인데
소음에 가려 먼지에 묻혀
안 들리고 사라져가리

너의 환호도
나의 탄식도
거기에 섞여 있겠지

Lattice

Painter Kim said "eyes are now open to the face and space,

But space-time is still overwhelming".

Once he fell in love with it,

He couldn't escape and got immersed.

It would be easy to understand if he draws it

Clearly with the same color and shape as before.

But it would be impossible for him to go back

Because he met a so wonderful and

Awe-inspiring world that he could not resist.

He must have been trapped in a space network.

It seems he is entangled in an ecstatic brain network.

I guess he's trapped there without knowing.

The inside of his grate is immesed in awe.

창살

면과 공간에는 이제 눈이 트이나
시공은 아직 버겁다던 김 화백
한번 거기에 푹 빠지더니
헤어나질 못하고 잠긴다

전처럼 쉬운 색깔과 모습으로
또렷또렷 그리면 얼마나
알기 쉽고 좋으련만
너무나 경이롭고 경외로운
떨칠 수 없는 세계를 만났기에
되돌아가기는 틀렸단다

우주망의 덫에 걸렸나보다
황홀한 뇌망腦網에 얽혀서 이리
저도 모르게 거기 갇혀 있나 봐
그의 창살 안은 경탄으로 잠겨 있다

Color and Picture

What your eyes see is color;

What you see in your brain is a picture.

What you hear is sound;

Music is what you hear in your brain.

What is seen

Shakes my heart;

What is heard

Makes my soul tremble.

There is a picture that is only visible to you

While watching together;

We listen together, but there is music

That can only be heard by me.

색깔과 그림

눈이 보는 건 색깔
뇌에 보이는 게 그림이지
귀가 듣는 건 소리
뇌에 들리는 게 음악이지

보이는 게
마음을 흔들지
들리는 게
영혼을 떨리지

함께 보는 데
너에게만 보이는 그림이 있지
같이 듣는데
나에게만 들리는 음악이 있다

High Tide

The sun sets.
You'll see a spectacular glow
Of a setting sun soon.
The violent wind is calming down.
The mud flat is now waiting for
The inflow of the tide.

When it is tilted, it becomes empty,
When it is empty,
You feel a sensible void.
What's empty is always
Refilled to be raised.

We tilt today and
Pour it out.
We fill up the void
With new stuff and
Redecorate tomorrow.

It is emptied as much as it is tilted,
Filled up as much as emptied, and
Will stand straight as much as it's filled.
You will be tilted and emptied
To be filled with abundance of joy
In greeting the rising tide of glory.

밀물

해가 기운다 곧
낙조의 장관을 보리
거세게 불던 바람이
잠잠해져 간다
갯벌은 이제
밀물을 기다리지

기울여야 비워지고
비어지면 허전하지
허전한 건 늘
새로 채워서
다시 일으키지

오늘을 기울여
쏟아버리고
비어 허전한 데를
새로 채워서
내일을 치켜세우지

기울인 만큼 비워지리
비운만큼 채워지지
채운 만큼 바로 서리
밀려드는 영광의 밀물을
풍성한 기쁨으로 맞이하게
비워서 허전하게 하리

A Silent Smile

He only smiles and is silent.
I notice that he is not ignoring me.
Even if I aske again, he only smiles.
Do I have to interpret it on my own?

I'm glad he doesn't scold or laugh at me.
His smile always pleases me and
It seems to say "don't worry, wait and see".
The time will come someday
when I can hear his voice.

I've been waiting for many years,
But I can't hear anything but smile.
Sometimes I feel like I can hear his voice,
But I'm furtively afraid I might mistake
my own voice for his.

말 없는 미소

미소만 짓고 말이 없다
무시하는 건 아닌 눈치다
다시 물어도 미소만 짓는다
알아서 해석하라는 건가

꾸짖거나 비웃지 않으니 다행이다
언제나 좋게 해주는 미소이니
걱정 말고 기다려 보라나 보다
언젠가는 목소리 들리는 때가 오리

오랜 세월 기다렸는데
미소뿐 말은 아직 안 들린다
가끔 들리는 듯한 때가 있는데
내 목소리를 그의 것으로
혹시 착각하나 슬며시 겁난다

제3부

The Tomorrow Within Today
오늘 안의 내일

Vines

Hearty vines

That will stretch out endlessly

From root to stem, and

From branch to leaf.

They are eternal runners

Who will bloom the flowers of glory.

They are earnest strings and beads

That connect heaven and earth,

And you and me.

These are ardent networks.

They are endless vines

That will bear the fruit of the promise.

덩굴

뿌리에서 줄기로
가지에서 잎으로
끝없이 뻗어나갈
정성 어린 덩굴들
영광의 꽃을 피워갈
영원할 러너들이지

하늘과 땅
너와 나를 이어주는
간절한 줄과 구슬들
절실한 네트워크들
약속의 열매를 맺을
무궁할 덩굴들이지

The Things That Live Inside You

You are not the only one
Who lives in you;
Genes that have been handed down
From the beginning are kept intertwined.

The bloody battles of survival,
The unforgettable joys and sorrows, and
Moments of wonder and awe that have been
Twisted and mingled from generation to generation,
Are living within you as countless pieces of life
Actually you are not you;
You're a complex of mind, thought and soul.

An unparalleled universe
Lives within you.
On this vine that will stretch out endlessly
What kind of trace do you want to leave?

네 안에 사는 것들

네 안에 사는 게
너만은 아니지
태초부터 내려온 유전자들이
주렁주렁 달려 간직되어 있지

생존의 피 싸움들
잊지 못할 애환들
경이와 경외의 순간들이
삶의 무수한 조각으로 대대로 꼬이고
섞이며 달려와 네 안에 살고 있지
실은 너는 네가 아니고
마음과 생각 영혼의 복합체이지

비길 데 없는 우주가
네 안에 살아간다
끝없이 벋어나갈 이 덩굴에
너는 어떤 자취를 남기려는가

Reserved Gifts

'It seems like I can see something now,
The clutter seems to have subsided.
I think I know something and
In the morning, I'll be one step ahead.'
I fell asleep with joy and thanks.

What happened!
It's different from yesterday.
There's only a thick fog outside the window.
'You're sitting on a present again,
You're really pretending to be a master!'

Hope is a reserved gift;
The reward will actually be awarded only
To the heart that'll appreciate and cherish it.
There will be no more gift to give to those
Who took it by themselves.

예비 된 선물

이제 무언가 보이는 듯 해
무엇인가 알 것도 같아
어수선한 게 잡히는 듯 해
아침이면 한 발짝 더 나가 있으리
기뻐 감사하며 잠에 들었지

어찌 된 일인가
어제와는 딴판이네
창밖이 자욱한 안개뿐이네
'또 선물을 깔고 앉았군,
주인인 체하는 게 몸에 뱄어!'

희망은 예비 된 선물
소중히 간직할 마음에게만
포상이 실제로 주어지리
스스로 잡아 챙긴 이에게
더 줄 선물은 없으리

Threat

Stripped street trees

Get wet in the winter rain;

Are they going to a recess

In the order of the flow?

Taking off your clothes

Doesn't mean to drive you out.

Where there is no renunciation,

There is no abandonment.

Nothing is deserted, but

There is a soul that gives up.

Threatening is to give you

A second chance.

It is to prepare the eyes

To see higher and deeper.

으름장

발가벗긴 가로수들이
겨울비에 젖는다
흐름의 질서를 따라
휴게에 들어가는 건가

옷을 벗기는 게
쫓아내는 건 아니리
포기가 없는 곳에
버림은 없으리
버려지는 것은 없고
단념하는 영혼이 있지

으름장을 늘어놓는 건
다음 기회를 주려는 거리
더 높이 더 깊이 볼
눈을 마련하라는 거지

Sunset

The sunset is the beginning of tomorrow,
When reflection inspires the will and
Plan checks the march.

How did you get hold of it?
Have you decided to hold onto it?
What looks and sounds are
passing by and coming?
The sighs fade away and
Cheers come rushing in.

There will be light and timely rain
That will make
The seed sown sprout.

해 질 녘

해 질 녘은 내일의 서막
성찰이 의지를 북돋아 주고
계획이 행진을 점검하는 때

붙들고 온 것은 어찌 되었나
붙잡고 갈 것을 결단하였나
어떤 모습들과 소리들이
스쳐가고 다가오는가
탄식은 멀리 사라져가고
환호성이 밀려 들어오리

뿌려지는 씨에
새싹을 돋아낼
빛과 단비가 내리리

A Weeping Willow

A weeping willow is dancing
While waiting at the crossing.
The loose hair is fluttering
In the December wind.

Perhaps it has received the light beam
That pierces through the clouds for a while
As a green light,
So the tree trembles with all its body and mind.
Brushing off the faded things that are still stuck,
It tries to hit the road.
'Somehow my feet don't come out!'

A weeping willow is dancing at the crossing;
Its heart is already running through the field.
Whether it knows or not that the road is planned,
It's overjoyed at the adventure it will cross over.

수양버들

건널목에서 기다리며
수양버들이 춤을 춘다
풀어헤친 머리카락이
섣달 바람에 휘날린다

구름을 비집고 잠시 쏟아내는
빛살을 청신호로 받아서인지
몸과 마음을 다해 요동친다
아직 달라붙은 바랜 것들을
훨훨 털어내고 길을 떠나려다
'어찌하나 발이 안 빠져나오네!'

건널목에서 춤추는 수양버들
마음은 벌써 벌판을 달리리
예정된 길인 걸 아는지 모르는지
넘고 건널 모험에 가슴 벅차리

Counting Chickens Before Hatched

'It's too hasty!
It's so stupid!'
Don't scold too much about
The counting chickens before hatched.

Are you running around to grab it?
Are you confident in your bright smile?
Do you want to wait patiently?
They are all about and about.
Who decides the turn and share?
Is prayer alone enough?

Expectations and rewards
Don't always go together.
We all pretend we're not and live by
'Counting chickens before hatched'.

김칫국

너무 조급하다고
너무 엉뚱하다고
핀잔주지 마세
김칫국부터 마시는 심정

설치며 잡아채려나
너털웃음에 자신만만한가
묵묵히 기다리려나
모두 오십 보 백 보이리
차례와 몫은 누가 정하나
기도만 가지고 충분할까

기대와 보상은 언제나
같이 가지는 않으리
우리는 모두 아닌척하며
김칫국부터 마시며 살지

Association

We met on the day
The wind blew and flowers bloomed,
So we'll meet again always on those days;
Because you left when the leaves were falling
On a rainy day
At times like that, your image comes out more clearly.

Even if it passed by,
Even if it was a momentary meeting,
Engraved in our hearts and souls,
We live together forever and ever.

O marvelous power of association
That links time to time!
Beautiful realm of associations
That put circuits between the minds!
Glory of endless associations
That weave souls and souls!

연상聯想

바람이 불고
꽃이 피던 날에 우리가 만났기에
그런 날이면 언제나 다시 만나지
비가 오던 날
잎이 지던 때에 떠났기에
그런 때면 너의 모습 더 짙게 돌아오지

훌쩍 지나갔어도
순간의 만남이었어도
마음과 영혼에 새겨져
언제나 어디까지나
한없이 함께 살아가지

시간에 시간을 고리 짓는
놀라운 연상의 힘이여!
마음 사이에 회로를 놓는
아름다운 연상의 나라여!
혼과 혼으로 망을 짜가는
끝없는 연상의 영광이여!

A Breather

To choose a step,
In the midst of silence,
To look ahead,
Everyone is taking a breather.

How can I catch only my breath?
I have to pick the speed of my heartbeat
And turn my thoughts too.
Turning is a choice.

The lungs suck in time,
Put it in the heart, and
Sprinkle it on the brain.
Everyone is busy choosing the time.

They all take a breather to change
The trajectory and try to catch the next axis.
No one can change the speed of time,
But everyone is allowed to set their paces.

숨 돌리기

걸음을 고르려
고요 가운데
앞길을 살피려
모두 숨 돌리기에 들어간다

어찌 숨만 돌리랴
박동도 고르고
생각도 돌려야지
돌리기는 고르기이지

폐가 시간을 빨아들여
심장에 담아주니
이를 다시 뇌에 뿌려준다
모두 시간 고르기에 바쁘다

궤도를 바꾸어 다음 축을 잡으려
모두 숨 돌리기를 하지
아무도 시간 속도를 바꿀 순 없으나
누구나 걸음 고르겐 허락되어 있으리

Rush

The world is in a rush.

What is your speed?

Do you know what the Earth's rotation speed is?

If you know the orbital speed, you will be more surprised.

Everyone has a given speed.

The faster the better for one,

And the slower the better for the other.

They each got their own right paces.

If you live in the middle of a race,

Speed becomes life.

When a means is mistaken for an end,

The tape is cut without knowing its meaning.

질주疾走

세상은 질주 가운데 있다
너의 속도는 얼마나 되나
지구의 자전 속도가 얼만지 아나
공전 속도를 알면 더 놀라리

저마다 주어진 속도가 있지
빠를수록 좋은 게 있고
느려야 좋은 게 있으리
각기 잘 맞는 걸음을 받았으리

경주 가운데 살아가다 보면
속도가 생명이 되기도 하지
수단이 목적으로 오인 되어서
의미도 모르고 테이프를 끊지

Two Pine Trees

Two pine trees are guarding
The entrance to a square
Where no one walks around
Early in a very cold morning.

They must have been pulled out
Of all others and planted here.
Medals hanging on the chest
Seem to be hard for them to handle.
Their backs are gradually bending
Due to job pressure on their shoulders.
Where they are looking,
What they are feeling,
What they are thinking,
They stand together, but they are alone.

Stand together,
But they have to stand alone;
Standing alone,
But they have to stand together.

소나무 두 그루

아무도 안 다니는
칼 추위 꼭두새벽인데
두 그루 소나무가
광장 입구를 지킨다

다른 이들을 다 제치고
뽑혀 와 심어졌으리
주렁주렁 가슴에 달린
훈장이 버거운 눈치다
어깨를 누르는 기대에
점점 등이 굽어져 간다
어디를 바라보는지
무엇을 느끼는지
무슨 생각을 하는지
같이 서 있으나 홀로이지

같이 서 있으나
홀로 서야 하고
홀로 서 있으나
같이 서야 하리

Miracle Day

You are still hesitating
To be held in that arms.
Since you've never seen
And touched in person,
How can you do that so quickly?

But, whether you remember it or not,
You must have experienced that amazing presence
Even for a very short moment.
It's the nation that you long for
Even when you hesitate.

How amazing it is
To wait without knowing!
Things beyond imagination
Will happen soon
On the day set by the miracle.

기적의 날

그 품에 안기기를
아직도 주저하지
직접 본 적 없고
못 만져봤으니
어찌 덥석 그러리

그러나 기억하건 못하건
아주 짧게나마 너는
그 놀라운 임재를 경험했으리
그곳은 머뭇거리면서도
네가 갈망하는 나라지

모르면서도 기다리니
얼마나 놀라운 일인가
상상을 넘는 일들이
곧 일어날 거야
기적이 정하는 날에

Betting

The dazzling sky is astonishing
As the warm wind of June
Pushes the clouds away.

Green waves ripple along the street
Decorated with flower baskets
And summer is growing up.

Greening trees are constantly
Absorbing light and busy
Forming tree rings.

The trees in the forest are
Arm-wrestling with the wind
And I'm betting on time.

내기

유월의 훈풍이
구름을 밀어내니
눈부신 하늘이 놀랍다

꽃들이 꾸민 가로로
초록 물결이 파도치며
여름이 자라 오른다

짙어가는 나무들은
끊임없이 빛을 빨아들여
나이테를 짓느라 바쁘다

숲속의 나무들은
바람과 팔씨름을 벌리고
나는 시간과 내기를 하고 있지

Who Is Like That?

The ideals and aspirations
As big as the universe
And as solemn as the heavens
Are turned over and smashed wholly
By a bad mood due to something
Smaller than millet.

Who is like that?
Will we be different tomorrow?

We shouted out that
We would give everything
For everyone.
But have we achieved anything good?
We pretend to be perfect alone,
But how does arrogance keep rising.

Who is such a person?
Will we get better tomorrow?

누가 그런가

우주같이 크고
하늘같이 엄숙한
이상과 포부가
좁쌀보다 작은 일에
기분이 상해 홀딱 뒤집혀
몽땅 박살 난다

누가 그런가
우리가 내일엔 좀 달라질까

모두를 위해
모두를 바친다고
우리가 큰소리치더니
제대로 이룬 게 무언가
우리는 홀로 완전한 척하는데
오만은 어찌 자꾸 솟구치나

그런 게 누군가
우리가 내일엔 좀 나아질까

The Tomorrow Within Today

Every living creature in the world
Soothes today's regrets with tomorrow's expectations,
Fills the empty space of unfulfilled aspirations
With the prayers that tomorrow will allow.

Amid countless waves,
In the unfathomable sea,
Particles are struggling,
Cells are fluttering,
Galaxies are tumbling.
They seem to live only for today,
But they hold on to the tomorrow that has been
Deeply ingrained into today and live in it.
They live today with the guarantee of tomorrow.
The root of today is tomorrow.

The tomorrow within today is truly wonderful;
This is a source of comfort we rely on without knowing it.
It is a cipher message that someone cherished within us.
But we can't decrypt it properly for the rest of our lives.

오늘 안의 내일

세상에 사는 모든 것들은
오늘의 아쉬움을 내일의 기대로 달래며
못 이룬 열망의 허전한 자리를
내일이 허락해줄 기원으로 채워가지

측량할 수 없는 바다
무수한 파도 가운데서
허덕이는 미립자들
설레는 세포들
요동치는 은하들
그들이 오늘만 사는 듯 보이나
오늘 안에 깊이 새겨 넣어준
내일을 붙잡고 그 안에 살아가지
내일을 담보하여 오늘을 살아간다
오늘의 뿌리는 내일이지

오늘 안의 내일은 진정 경이롭다
이는 우리가 모르면서도 의지하는
위로의 원천이지
우리 안에 누군가 소중히 간직해준 암호메시지인데
우리는 이를 평생 제대로 해독 못하며 살아가지

Search For Life

As the space race begins,

The search for life heats up.

For some reason, their enthusiasm is great.

They depart with confidence without evidence.

I hope that the endless passion to find life

Is not a slave to the powers of the world.

Is pure curiosity the origin of this passion?

Is an irresistible longing the source of this attempt?

Whose slave is curiosity?

Is longing a slave to what?

The body picks stars from space and

The soul seeks life from heaven.

생명 찾기

우주 경쟁이 시작되면서
생명 찾기 시도가 열을 올린다
무슨 동기에서인지 열정이 대단하다
안 보이지만 찾을 거라 믿고 떠나지

생명 탐색의 끝없는 열정이
세상 권력의 노예가 아니길 바라네
순수한 호기심이 이 열정의 발단인가
떨칠 수 없는 그리움이 이 시도의 원천인가

호기심은 누구의 노예인가
그리움은 무엇의 노예인가
몸은 우주에서 별을 따고
혼은 하늘에서 생명을 추구하지

Shadow World

A snowstorm blew on the path
Where the leaves were flying,
And now the petals fall.

Petals fly and sit on the path
Embroidered by shadows.
Shadows gather and play.
What kind of conversation do they have?
Is it past joy and sorrow,
Or the expectation of future?

Is the visible
the shadow of the invisible?
Aren't the stars seen from deep space
The shadows of the past?
In the eyes of a far away star,
Our current earth may be seen
As a shadow of the past?

Our angels in heaven.
Are we their shadows?
Are they our shadows?

그림자 세상

잎이 날리던 길로
눈발이 불어치더니
지금 꽃잎이 날린다

그림자들이 수놓는 길로
꽃잎이 날아와 앉는다
그림자들이 모여서 논다
어떤 대화를 그들은 나누나
지나온 애환인가
기대의 미래인가

보이는 것은 실로
안 보이는 것의 그림자인가
심 우주에서 보는 별은
사라진 옛 그림자 아닌가
지금 여기도 먼 별나라에서는
이미 지나간 그림자가 아닐까

하늘에 사는 우리의 천사들
우리가 그들의 그림자인가
그들이 우리의 그림자일까

An Icy Road

An afternoon on a day of heavy snow
Greeted spring amid a snowy scene,
And overnight, the strong cold winds
Turned the streets into icy roads.

Cars rushing to work at dawn are
Lining up waiting for a green light.
Whether you know the dangers of ice or not,
You have to run when the signal comes.

Though it was yesterday that I slipped,
Tangled and bumped into trouble,
I firmly believe such a thing won't happen to me.
Where does such confidence come from?

In line with the green signal,
The vehicles are pushed in time and rushing down the road.
Without knowing the moment ahead,
They run at full speed in an unknown area.

빙판

함박눈 내리던 날의 오후가
설경 가운데 봄을 맞더니
밤사이 강추위 거센 바람에
거리는 빙판으로 변했지

서두는 새벽 출근 차량들이
청신호를 기다리며 줄 서 있다
빙판의 위험을 알건 모르건
신호가 떨어지면 달려야 하리

미끄러져 엉키고 부딪치며
곤욕을 치른 게 어제인데
그런 건 내겐 아니지 굳게 믿지
어디서 나오는 자신감일까

청신호에 맞추어 차량들이
시간에 밀려갈 길을 재촉한다
순간의 앞도 전혀 알지 못하며
미지의 영역을 전속으로 달린다

Spring

Spring does not come just on
The fist day of spring.
A blizzard may strike with
A sharp wind on the day.

Some houses are already in spring,
For some spring is coming soon,
And some do not know when.

It enters a house with an open door,
And walks past a closed house.
Spring comes when it desires to come,
And goes into the house waiting for it.

입춘

입춘이라고 오늘 바로
봄이 들어오겠나
칼바람에 눈보라가
덮치기도 하지

봄이 이미 온 집도 있고
곧 들어올 집도 있고
언제일지 모르는 집도 있지

대문이 열린 집엔 들어오고
닫힌 집은 지나쳐 가리
봄은 오고 싶을 때 오고
기다리는 집에 들어가리

Momentum

Just yesterday, I didn't think that
The flower buds would come out and do a good job,
But today they are already in full bloom.
It's the ability of an incomprehensible power
That has been hidden.

Everything changes in an instant.
It is truly an astonishing expansion.
The compressed power springs up
And a powerful driving force erupts.
It blooms amazingly with momentum.
When the momentum is broken, it will soon wither.

Every gesture that rises, endures,
And descends is surfing with momentum.
Where does the momentum come from?
The wondrous principles that govern the world
Will flow from the source of awe.

기세

어제만 해도 꽃망울이
비집고 나와 제구실할까
여겨지지 않더니
오늘 벌써 활짝 폈다
숨어 도사린 불가해한 힘의 능력이다

모든 게 순간에 달라진다
진정 경탄할 팽창이다
압축된 동력이 튀어 오르며
세찬 추진력이 분출한다
여세 몰이로 놀랍게 피어난다
기세가 꺾이면 곧 시들게 되리

오르고 버티다 내려가는 모든
몸짓은 기세를 타는 서핑이지
타력은 어디서 누가 보내는가
세상을 다스리는 경이로운 원리는
경외의 원천에서 흘러나오리

제4부

The Tunnel of Waves
파도의 터널

The Tunnel of Waves

This is not a tunnel where we tremble
In fear of losing everything,
It's the pathway of aspirations we pass
Through to reach the pinnacle of our lives.

This is not the big wave
We tremble for fear of losing everyone,
It's a surf-riding where we run with
Excitement to seize the climax moment.

파도의 터널

이는 모든 걸 잃을까 봐
두려워 떠는 터널이 아니라
필생의 정점을 찍으려
스치는 열망의 통로이지

이는 모두를 놓칠까 봐
무서워 떠는 큰 파도가 아니라
절정의 순간을 잡으려
설레며 달려가는 파도타기이지

Games and Rites

We come from there,

We play games,

And after the ceremony

We go back there.

How are you going to bet on what to win?

What kind of flag do you display

To decorate the stage with,

And what kind of ritual do you want to end?

Is this a game you accidentally caught?

Is it your favorite game?

Is it a game that you are to follow?

Is it your own stage?

The whole world is in the midst of a star-picking game,

And a ceremony to ride a flower cart.

The whole land becomes a busy whirlpool

With a parade of games and rites.

게임 그리고 예식

거기에서 와서
게임 하다가
예식을 마치고
그리로 돌아가지

무얼 걸고 무얼 따려고
어떻게 게임을 벌이는가
무슨 깃발로 무대를 장식하여
어떤 예식으로 막을 내리려나

얼떨결에 잡은 게임인가
제가 좋아 고른 게임인가
시키는 대로 따르는 게임인가
나름대로 꾸미는 무대인가

온 세상이 별을 따는 게임
꽃수레 타는 예식 중에 있다
게임 그리고 예식의 퍼레이드로
온 땅은 바쁜 소용돌이가 되지

A Bridle

The prisoners of time, and
The slaves of money,
Pass by in procession.

Who is not a slave?
Aren't we all prisoners?
We wore a bridle that we couldn't take off.

In order not to be a lost child,
You have to turn on time, and
You can't go out of track.

Lush trees wither without notice,
And long-awaited festivals
Are often cancelled in vain.

Still, we keep planting trees and
Everyone looks forward to all the festivals.
Isn't this also a preordained bridle?

굴레

시간의 포로들
돈의 노예들
행렬 지어 지나간다

누가 노예가 아닐까
모두 포로가 아닌가
우리는 벗을 수 없는 굴레를 썼지

기아가 안 되려면
시간에 맞추어 돌아야지
궤도를 벗어날 수 없지

무성하던 나무가 예고 없이
시들어지고 대망의 축제가
허무하게 무산되기도 하지

그래도 우리는 나무를 계속 심고
축제를 모두 손꼽아 기다리지
이 또한 예정된 굴레가 아닌가

Life Cycle

The sudden release of a flash is
A death explosion that marks
The end of a supernova.

But this is just
Part of the life cycle.
Not everything you can't see is dead.

The rare and precious material that arises from
The agony of death will be ejected into space
To create a new generation of stars.

The galaxy rotates endlessly,
The stars and we also revolve
In infinite orbits along the life cycle.

생명주기

돌연한 섬광의 발산은
초신성의 마지막을 알리는
죽음의 폭발이지

그러나 이것은 다만
생명주기의 한 부분이리
안 보이는 게 다 죽은 건 아니지

단말마의 고통에서 생겨나는
진귀한 소재는 우주로 분출되어
새 세대 별들을 만들어가리

은하가 끝없이 선회한다
별들도 우리도 생명주기를 따라
한없는 궤도를 돌아가지

The Root of Soul

The invisible and unmeasurable powers
Are governing the visible and
Accessible universe unwittingly.

An unfathomable unconscious world
Rules over our lives by occupying
The depths that cannot be grasped.

Dark energy is the source of powers,
Containing the beginning of the beginning,
Where the nucleus of the universe resides.

The realm of the unconscious is the place
Where the source of life is recorded,
And the root of soul is established.

영혼의 뿌리

안 보이고 잴 수도 없는 힘이
보이고 접근할 수 있는 우주를
모르는 사이에 다스려 간다

헤아릴 수 없는 무의식세계가
잡히지 않는 깊은 속을 차지하여
우리의 삶을 지배해 가지

암흑에너지는 힘의 원천
시작의 시작이 담겨 있는
우주의 중추가 사는 곳

무의식의 영역은 삶의 원천
자초지종이 기록되어 있는
영혼의 뿌리가 내려진 곳

Raindrops

The rain lit by street lamps at night
Is exceptionally fantastic
The dance of raindrops is seen
In the flickering rays of light

In the fine movement of a tiny raindrop,
You can see countless fine particles
Vibrating in it without knowing
Whether it is night or day.

Too big to see,
Too small to see,
Enigmatically beautiful universes
Live in hiding.

All in the universe is wriggling
In the rain in the rays of light.
When, where, and what do they want to catch?
What conversations are they having?

빗방울

밤 가로등이 비춰주는
빗발은 유난히 환상적이다
흔들리는 빛살 가운데서
빗방울들의 무도가 보인다

아주 작은 빗방울들의 미동
그 안에서 밤인지 낮인지도
모르며 진동하는 무수한
미세입자들까지 보인다

너무 커서 안 보이는
아주 작아 보이지 않는
놀랍게 아름다운
나라들이 숨어 산다

빛살 안의 빗발 가운데서
우주의 모두가 꿈틀거린다
어느 때 어디서 무얼 잡으려는지
무슨 대화를 그들은 나누고 있는지

Living World

Grass and flowers cover the mountains and fields,

And the blue sky is always dazzling.

The wind blows in between them.

We all believe that

The whole world is alive,

So we sing a song to live.

Who would believe that

The whole world is dead,

And play a game of death?

Even if our thoughts and feelings are different

And our paths are different,

We hope to reach the same destination.

The wind blows endlessly

To harmonize the song and the game,

And the sky is still high and bright today.

살아 있는 세상

풀과 꽃은 산과 들을 덮고
푸른 하늘은 늘 눈부시지
그 사이를 바람이 불어 채운다

우리는 세상 모두가
살아 있다고 믿기에
사는 노래를 부르지

누가 세상 모두를
죽어 있다고 믿기에
죽는 게임을 하랴

생각과 느낌이 다르고
가는 길이 달라도
이르는 데는 같길 바라지

노래와 게임이 어우러지도록
바람이 끝없이 불어 들어온다
하늘은 오늘도 높고 찬란하다

A Rosebush

On the street where May is ripening,
A rosebush has gained a world
Shaking the splendid figure,
It raises the head and chest.

It radiates color and fragrance
In an effort to reach someone
Who will be somewhere high and far away.

Are you struggling because
Your feet are tied and you can't run?
Sadness comes when you know you are tied up.

Whether we're crawling, running, or flying,
Everyone is living in a given frame.
But why are you making such a great fuss alone?
Someone is looking down sadly.

장미꽃 나무

오월이 익어가는 거리에
장미가 한 세상을 얻었다
화려한 모습을 뒤흔들며
머리와 가슴을 치켜세운다

빛깔과 향기를 뿜어댄다
높이 멀리 어딘가에 있을
누군가를 만나고 싶어서리

발이 묶여 달려가지 못해
안타까이 발버둥을 치는가
묶인 걸 알 때 슬픔이 오리

기거나 뛰거나 날거나 모두
주어진 틀에 동여매여 살고 있지
그런데 무얼 그렇게 홀로 법석을 떠는가
누군가 너를 안쓰럽게 내려다보고 있으리

A Lifetime

We wander all over the world
To catch things that are not in the world.
The biggest,
The highest, or
The most valuable.

They don't look stupid,
But they can't help it.
Someone is pulling them somewhere,
But they don't know where, and
They don't know who it is.

We struggle all our lives,
Trying to do the impossible.
Are we holding something wrong?
We may get lost somewhere.
Have we been deceived by someone?

한평생

세상에 없는 걸 잡으려
우리는 온 세상을 헤맨다
가장 큰 것
가장 높은 곳
가장 값진 것

어리석게 안 보이는데
어쩔 수 없어 그러나보다
어디서 누군가 끄는데
어디인지 모르지
누구인지 모르리

이룰 수 없는 걸 해내려
한평생을 허덕거린다
무언가를 잘못 잡고 있어선가
어디선가 길을 잃어서리
누군가의 속임에 빠져선가

Wonder

How beautiful!
Your smiling face,
Your gaze, and
Your kind heart.
We'll always be together.
We're afraid each of us will leave.

How wonderful!
Our meeting,
Our affair, and
Our farewell.
Who does this?
What's next?

How sublime!
Our flower,
Our star, and
Our universe.
They'll unfold limitlessly.
They'll run endlessly.

경이

얼마나 아름다운가
당신의 미소 짓는 얼굴
바라보는 눈빛
다정한 마음
우리는 언제나 함께하리
우리는 각기 떠날까봐 두렵지

얼마나 경이로운가
우리의 만남
우리의 사귐
우리의 작별
누가 이렇게 하나
다음은 어떻게 되나

얼마나 숭고한가
우리의 꽃
우리의 별
우리의 우주
한없이 펼쳐지지
끝없이 달려가리

Already

It has already passed,

But in vain, will you try to get it back?

You should hold on to what will be.

It's already broken,

Are you recklessly trying to fix it?

You have to get a new bowl.

It's already over,

Do you only want to look back and mourn?

You have to start over.

Do you want to do something alone

With all your heart and sweat?

There's nothing in the world you can do alone.

이미

이미 지나갔는데
헛되이 돌이켜 보려나
될 것을 붙들어야지

이미 깨졌는데
무모하게 붙여보려나
새 그릇을 마련해야지

이미 끝났는데
뒤만 돌아보고 애통만 하려나
다시 시작을 해야지

온몸 다해 피땀 흘려
무언 갈 홀로 해보려는가
혼자 할 수 있는 건 세상에 없지

The Kingdom of Stars (1)

Thoughts that fathom the stars, and
Hearts that want to win them,
Catch their breaths
To the beat and
Run along the windy riverside
Today, too.

Have you now found true rest
In the kingdom of stars you dreamed of?
Yesterday's thoughts are
not today's thoughts,
And today's heart
Will be different tomorrow.

The kingdom of stars is
The tomorrow that lives within us.
It's the image of tomorrow
Reflected in today.
It's a twinkle
That's hard to catch.

별나라 (1)

별을 헤아리는 생각들
별을 따고 싶은 마음들
박동에 맞추어
숨을 가다듬으며
바람 부는 강변을
오늘도 달려간다

꿈꾸던 별나라에서
이제 안식을 얻었나
어제의 생각은
오늘의 생각이 아니요
오늘의 마음이
내일은 달라지리

별나라는
우리 안에 사는 내일
오늘 안으로 비친
내일의 모습
붙잡기 어려운
반짝임이지

The Kingdom of Stars (3)

As a friend who leads and protects,
You and I go together while looking at the stars.
To overcome and embrace all,
We live together while waiting for the stars.

In the visible kingdom of stars,
Our joys and sorrows pile up like snow.
In the invisible star kingdom,
Our next will be written down.

The visible kingdom of stars is our heritage.
The invisible world is our future kingdom.
Someone has done this, and
It is marvelous in our eyes.*

* Psalm 118:23

별나라 (3)

이끌고 지켜주는 친구이기에
별나라를 바라보며 함께 가지
모두를 이겨주고 안겨주기에
별나라를 기다리며 함께 살지

보이는 별나라 안에
우리의 애환이 눈처럼 쌓여가지
안 보이는 별나라 안에
우리의 다음이 기록되어 가리

보이는 별나라는 우리의 유산
안 보이는 별나라가 우리의 미래 왕국
누군가 이렇게 만들었으리
우리는 놀라워 바라볼 뿐이지*

* 시편 118: 23

Resentment

We hope, therefore we are disappointed.
We believe, therefore we are resentful.

Is there anyone in the world who is not disappointed?
Who will live in the world without resentment?

Everyone is disappointed and resentful,
Because everyone has hope and faith.

Are you going to disobey because the answer is slow?
You should know that love flows even in silence.

원망

바라기에 실망하지
믿기에 원망하지

세상에 실망 않는 이 있나
누가 원망 없이 세상을 살랴

누구나 실망하고 원망하며 사니
모두가 소망과 믿음이 있어서지

대답이 느리다고 거역할 건가
침묵 속에서도 사랑은 흐르지

The Beast

Don't be sad that
You were rejected.
Don't be so mad at
Being blocked.
Isn't it only a stick
that tames animals?

Do you adore
The crushing force?
Reckless dash is
A rhino's specialty.
Isn't it wisdom to know
How to retreat?

We have to be wary of the beast
That lives inside us.
Even your head sometimes
Wobbles with animal spirits.
How can we spoil great designs
With shameful animal instincts?

짐승

거절당했다고
서러워 마라
차단당하는 걸
너무 노여워 마라
이는 오직 짐승을 길들이는
막대기 아니겠느냐

파죽지세를
흠모하시나
무모한 돌진은
코뿔소의 특기이지
물러설 줄 아는 게
지혜 아니겠는가

내 안에 사는
짐승을 경계해야지
네 머리도 때론
혈기로 뒤뚱거리지
부끄러운 동물본능으로
어찌 대사를 망치랴

Riding Together

Carried by the warm wind of June,
Summer rushes in.
Following the footsteps of time,
The shade of trees is getting deeper.

When the wind blows,
The branches sway,
And fear creeps
Into the joy of pride.

We live even without motion sickness
On the frantically spinning Earth.
It will be so because we ride together and run.
The bigger the vehicle, the better.

If you stay in it,
You won't be shaken.
If you hide in it
You won't be afraid.

동승同乘

유월의 훈풍에 실려
여름이 밀려들어 오고
시간의 발길을 따라
녹음이 짙어져 간다

바람이 불어치면
가지들은 요동하고
뿌듯하던 기쁨 안으로
두려움이 서려온다

정신없이 회전하는 지구에서
우리는 멀미도 없이 살아가지
동승하여 달리니 그렇게 되리
큰 차를 탈수록 더 그러하리

그 안에 있으면
흔들리지 않으리
그 안에 숨으면
두렵지 않으리

Gamblers

Big or small,

Like it or not,

Everyone gambles

All are gamblers.

The bigger the stake,

The higher the tension,

The more exiting,

The more people flock to it.

On the money board rather than the sports games,

On the war board rather than the political game,

Money, honor, power gamblers,

Drooling, place their bets.

What are you gambling today?

How much did you win and lose yesterday?

What is tomorrow's gamble?

Are the game preparations going well?

The biggest gamble is

A game for life.

Isn't life more precious than the world?

Who do you trust and where do you bet?

도박꾼

크건 작건
좋든 싫든
누구나 도박을 하지
모두 도박꾼이다

판돈이 클수록
긴장도가 높을수록
흥미진진할수록
사람들이 모여들지

스포츠게임보다는 돈판에
정치 게임보다는 전쟁판에
군침 흘리며 돈 명예 권력형
도박꾼들이 내기를 걸지

오늘은 무슨 도박을 하나
어제는 얼마를 따고 잃었나
내일의 도박은 무엇으로 결정했나
너의 게임 준비는 잘되어가고 있나

가장 큰 도박은
생명을 건 게임이리
생명이 천하보다 귀하지 않은가
누굴 믿고 어디에 내기를 걸건가

A Name

They are all carried away
By the wind and
Disappear over the horizon.

Everyone should call
The living name,
Not the dead name.

Everyone should be given
A name to live,
Not a name to die.

이름

모두 바람에 실려
지평 너머로
사라져 간다

모두 죽은 이름이
아니라
살아 있는 이름을 불러야지

누구나 죽을 이름이
아니라
살 이름을 받아야지

The Time Bound Feet

Clouds flow in

Where the wind blows.

The soft rain gently strokes flower buds

and on a surprisingly sunny day,

The petals are in full bloom.

How are your days blooming?

Has your longing

Now found a place to rest

As you dreamed

And waited?

Whether you succeed

Or fail,

You are the time bound feet,

Rain or wind,

You must run and pass by.

시간에 묶인 발

바람이 부는 데로
구름이 흘러들어오고
보슬비가 꽃망울을 쓰다듬으니
놀랍게 화창한 날이
꽃잎을 활짝 피운다

바라보던 너의 날은
어떻게 피어가는가
너의 그리움은 이제
꿈꾸며 기다리던 대로
안식할 데를 얻었나

네가 이루거나
못 이루거나
너는 시간에 묶인 발이니
비가 오나 바람이 부나
너는 달려 지나가야 하리

Beginning

Are the years passing by in vain?

Time passes as promised.

If you go there knowing that it is the end,

The beginning will wait there.

I doubt the promise,

So the day we meet is far away.

시작

세월이 덧없이 스쳐 가는가
약속대로 흘러가는 거리

끝인 줄 알고 가보면
시작이 거기서 기다리지

기약을 의심하기에
만날 날이 아득해 지리

제5부

The Teacup and the Sea
찻잔과 바다

The Sound Inside Me

I hear the voice
inside me.

Is it my voice
that I have built up,
or a voice that resounds
from a place I can't reach?

Even though I'm not certain,
I hold on tight to this and run.

내 안의 소리

깊이서 들려오는
내 안의 소리

내가 다져 넣은
나의 소리일까
닿을 수 없는 데서
울려오는 목소리이리

갸우뚱하면서도
꼭 붙들고 달리지

Delicate Signs

You urged it like that,
and there was a reason.
It's not like you know it,
but what did you notice?

When the blink of an eye comes in,
my heart shakes and
my body catches it and runs.
Collecting and refining
incoming hints,
I will design tomorrow.

That's the feeling!
I can't see or hear it,
but a web of dialogue woven with delicate signs
truly turns heaven and earth.

낌새

그렇게 재촉하더니
이유가 있었구먼
알고 그런 건 아닌 듯싶은데
그래도 무슨 낌새를 챘으리

눈짓이 들어오니
마음이 흔들리고
몸이 받아 달려가지
들어오는 낌새들을
모으고 가다듬어
내일을 설계해 간다

바로 그거지 그 느낌!
안 보이고 안 들리지만
낌새로 엮어지는 대화의 망이
하늘과 땅을 실로 돌려가지

Fidgets

A woman waving her clothes in the wind
and hovering around at the bus stop
tilts her head and snoops.
Impatient is waiting for the bus.

I wonder where she's going
to meet someone for what.
Is she excited about good news,
or anxious for bad things?
Is it a habit of impatience?

It will come when the time is right,
so why is she in such a hurry?
Does she try to cheer up the joy of meeting,
or want to put her heavy load down quickly?

Everyone is nervous.
Waiting is in a big rush.
Looking forward to it, you are fidgety;
As it's coming soon, I grow restless;
There's hope, so you're impatient.

조바심

바람에 옷자락 날리며
정류장에서 서성대는 아낙네
고개를 빼 기웃거린다
조바심이 버스를 기다린다

무얼 하러 누구를 만나러
어디로 가는지 궁금하다
좋은 일로 들떠 선가
나쁜 일로 마음 졸이나
습관이 된 조급증인가

때가 되면 올 터인데
어찌 그리 서두르는가
만남의 기쁨을 북돋우려 선가
짐을 빨리 내려놓고 싶어 서리

모두가 조바심친다
기다림이 서두른다
기대하니 마음 졸이지
곧 다가오리니 안절부절못한다
희망이 있으니 조바심치지

Hump and Bend

In the midst of the hurdles and turns
of survival and life, our rivers flow.
Overcoming hurdles and
following the meandering flow,
our tomorrow unfolds.

Our lives and songs,
and texts and drawings
are also endlessly transformed
in the whirlpool of change
with the passage of time.

Our life is a long river
with endless humps and bends.
In the endless vortex of evolution,
everyone is always trying to seize something.
What are you going to hold on to?

고비와 굽이

생존과 생활의
고비와 굽이 가운데로
우리의 강은 흐르고
고비를 넘고 굽이를 돌며
우리의 내일은 펼쳐져 가지

우리의 삶과 노래
글과 그림도
시간의 흐름을 타고
변화의 소용돌이 속에
끝없이 탈바꿈을 해간다

우리의 삶은 끝없는
고비와 굽이의 긴 강
한없는 진화의 회오리 안에서
모두 무언갈 늘 붙들려 하지
무엇을 잡아 어찌 하려는가

Contestants

Players pay attention closely
to the signal of the start
from the earth and the sky, and
from the inside and the outside.

In order not to miss anything,
they gather their hearts and souls
to grab something.
They are all keenly poised.

We are all contestants
waiting for the signal.
Is it a game to be played as a start,
or a contest to be played as a finish?

경기자

땅에서 하늘에서
안에서 밖에서
시작을 알리는 신호에
경기자들이 눈독 들인다

놓치지 않으려
무언 갈 잡아채려
마음과 혼을 모은다
태세를 갖춘다

우리는 모두 경기자
신호를 기다린다
시작처럼 할 경기일까
마무리처럼 할 경기일까

Wall Clock

A child who fell in love with a clock pendulum
made the pendulum stop accidentally
while playing with the wall clock.

Surprised, the child ran to the mother.
The relief pitcher, who was smiling while looking at the situation, stroked the child.
"My child has a knack for stopping time!"

When the mother set the wall clock and
pulled the pendulum and released it,
the rhythm of time begins again.
'My mom has the skills to revive time!'

Mom has long since passed away.
When her child's time stops here,
will the mother come running to revive the child's time?

벽시계

시계추에 반한 아이가
벽시계를 붙들고 놀다가
그만 뒤뚱 추가 멈춰 섰다

놀라서 엄마한테 달려갔지
사태를 바라보며 미소 짓던
구원투수가 쓰다듬어주며
"우리 애는 시간도 멈추는 재주가 있네!"

벽시계를 바로잡아 세우고
추를 잡아당겼다 놓아주니
시간의 율동이 다시 시작된다
'우리 엄마는 시간을 되살리는 기술도 있네!'

엄마는 그곳으로 가신 지 오래지
아이의 여기 시간이 뒤뚱 멈출 때
엄마는 아이시간을 소생시키려 달려올까

A Move

I'm moving from a town

I know well

to a place I know no one.

Every day is a moving day,

but I'm sure I'll be

bothered by it.

Are you afraid of what kinf of place it is?

You have friends wherever you go,

but are you worried about who to hang out with?

I'm looking forward to a place to move.

How much would it be better there than here?

It would be incomparably better there.

When I relocate, the emotion of

the burning sunset enjoyed here will be followed

by the joy of the brilliant morning glow.

이사

잘 아는 동네에서
아무도 모르는 곳으로
이사를 간다

하루하루가
이사 가는 날이라지만
아무래도 마음 쓰게 되지

어떤 곳일까 거기가 두려운가
어디에 가도 친구는 있다지만
누구와 지내야 할지 걱정인가

이사 갈 집에 기대를 걸어본다
여기보다 거기가 얼마나 더 좋을까
비교할 수 없이 거기가 좋겠지

여기서 누리던 불타는 낙조의 감동은
이사하는 날
찬란한 아침놀의 환희로 이어지게 되리

Circuit Turn

Blowing the last of September,
the cold wind shakes the sky and the earth,

Riding the clouds and being carried into the river, yesterday's heart makes today cry.

Is it a problem of inequity, a matter of existence,
a desire of the body, or a plea of the soul?

Are you betting on the days to come
because you regret the unfulfilled days of the past?

So everyone goes around the circuit
to practice celebrating victory.

회로 돌기

구월의 끝자락을 날리며
찬바람이 하늘과 땅을 흔든다

구름을 타고 강물에 실려
어제의 마음이 오늘을 울먹인다

불공평의 불만인가 존재의 문제인가
육체의 욕구인가 영혼의 간구인가

못다 한 지난날이 아쉬워
다가올 날에 내기를 거는가

그래서 모두 회로를 돌며
승리 축하 연습을 하는 거지

Flying the Flag

Athletes are filling the amphitheater
with colorful flags.

Who is the flag for?
What do you want to show with the flag?
How are you going to display your flag?

You have planted and grown a lot.
The fruit should be well harvested.

Are the players trying to win medals
giving everything to the flag,
or are the flag and you separate?

Winners cheer and losers struggle.
Do you want to end your life with this?

What did you get from this event?
When you come back and fall deep alone,
what fills your mind?

깃발을 날리며

형형색색의 깃발을 날리며
원형경기장을 메우는 선수들

누구를 위한 깃발인가
무얼 보이려는 깃발인가
어떻게 날리려는 깃발인가

심고 키운 건 많은데
열매를 잘 따내야지

메달을 거머쥐려는 무리
깃발에 모두를 바치나
깃발은 깃발 너는 너인가

승자는 환호 패자는 몸부림
평생을 이걸로 끝맺으려나

이 행사로 무얼 얻었나
돌아와 홀로 깊이 잠길 때
가슴에는 무엇이 차오르나

Fishing Without Bait

The meaning of fishing without bait
is to catch that time
in the long-awaited sea.

I hang a fishing line with a float
on a sturdy fishing rod
and wait while watching.

There are things in the world you can't catch with bait.
If you're willing to sacrifice everything you have to catch it,
you're not actually catching it, you're being caught by it.

I won't be troubled by swarms of sharks,
I won't get caught up in the whale fights.
I'll focus my attention to the sign of the time.

I cast a fishing line without bait
and watch intently.
I was caught without realizing it.

곧은 낚시질

곧은 낚시를 내리는 뜻은
대망의 바다에서
그 시간을 낚으려 서지

든든한 낚싯대에
낚시찌를 달아 드리우고
바라보며 기다린다

세상엔 미끼로 잡을 수 없는 게 있지
갖고 있는 모두를 바쳐 잡으려는 건
실은 잡기보다 거기에 잡혀서이지

상어 떼 추격을 두려워 않고
고래 싸움에 휘말리지 않으리
시간의 표적에 촉각을 곤두세우리

곧은 낚시를 드리우고
골똘히 지켜본다
저도 모르게 잡혀서이지

The Teacup and the Sea

The visible world is a teacup,
and the invisible universe is the sea.
The world that the intellect touches is a teacup,
and the domain that the intellect cannot reach is the sea.

How can I see
where I can't see?
What can make you reach
when you can't?

Is it a game of the dimension of putting the sea
in a teacup to see beyond and touch it?
The teacup eagerly explores a way to win the game.
Will the sea allow the game to go well?

The day the teacup is inflated, it will contain the sea.
When the sea shrinks, it can be put in a teacup.
Everything is possible in the realm of imagination.
But no one knows when it will actually happen.

The visible comes from the invisible,
and the invisible lives in the visible.

찻잔과 바다

보이는 세상은 찻잔
안 보이는 우주는 바다
지성이 닿는 세계는 찻잔
지성이 못 닿는 영역은 바다

안 보이는 곳은
어떻게 보게 될까
못 닿는 때는
무엇이 닿게 해주나

너머를 보게 되고 닿게 되는 게
바다를 찻잔에 담는 차원의 게임인가
찻잔은 이길 방법을 골똘히 탐색하리
바다가 게임이 잘되게 허락을 해줄까

찻잔이 팽창되는 날 바다를 담게 되리
바다가 수축하는 때 찻잔에 담기게 되지
상상의 영역에서는 모든 게 가능하지
언제 실제 일어날지는 아무도 모르지

보이는 것은 안 보이는 데서 나오고
안 보이는 것이 보이는 것 속에 살지

Network

If you look closely,
all the roads
are connected.

Wherever we live,
people are meant to communicate
with each other.

I don't know why,
but this sophisticated network
will do amazing things.

Circuits sprout from the breath.
A gigantic network of beats arises.
All is alive and dancing wonderfully.

네트워크

자세히 살펴보면
길은 모두
연결되어 있고

언제 어디서 살든
사람은 서로
통하게 되어 있지

왜인지는 모르지만
이 정교한 네트워크가
놀라운 뜻을 이루어가리

숨결에서 회로가 돋아나온다
박동의 거대한 네트워크가 생겨난다
모두가 살아 멋진 춤을 춘다

Zenith

The pinnacle of beauty
that shakes the soul is
the zenith of imagination
that the yearning gropes for.

As the wind blows away the dust,
a marvelous light reveals the wave height.
The shape of the climax will change
depending on what you see,
how it sounds,
and why it comes and touches you.

Rising to the peak of a moment,
you will feel the pulse of eternity;
Standing at the pinnacle of a point,
you will hear the breath of infinity.

절정

영혼을 흔드는
아름다움의 절정은
그리움이 더듬는
상상의 극치이지

바람이 먼지를 벗겨내니
놀라운 빛이 파고를 드러낸다
무엇이 보이는지
어떻게 들리는지
왜 와서 닿는지 따라
절정의 모습은 달라지리

한때의 절정에 올라
영원의 맥박을 느끼리
한 점의 극치에 서서
무한의 숨결을 들으리

Playground

It's crazy to tear down a flawless
children's playground with heavy equipment.
It has been remodeled according to the trend of the times.
How do antiques fit into a new day?

Children's playgrounds follow the adults,
and the adult playground becomes children's.
A game that competes for dimensions dances dizzyingly.
A changing world will change their choices.

The world nurtures them
and they transform the world.
The water becomes the river,
and the river becomes the way of the water.

놀이터

멀쩡한 어린이 놀이터를
중장비로 뜯어내느라 법석이다
시대사조에 따라 개조한단다
골동품이 어찌 새날에 맞으랴

어린이 놀이터는 어른을 바짝 따르고
어른 놀이터는 어린이처럼 되어가지
차원을 다투는 게임이 어지러이 춤춘다
변하는 세상이 이들의 선택을 바꾸리

그들을 세상이 키워가고
세상을 그들이 개조해가지
물이 강을 이루어가고
강은 물의 길이 되어가지

Sheepish Smile

Angry eyes,

Eyes of doubt.

Begging eyes,

Where are you wandering outside the iron bars?

No matter how wide you open

your eyes and stare intently,

there is nothing caught in the dark.

Only a desperate imagination

sends signals and measures the depth.

There is no response even when the ball is thrown.

Is there anyone who can get it out there?

Where has the person disappeared?

Is the recipient judging the time to answer?

How many unanswered questions

are there in the world?

You know you'll get it,

so you keep sending the signal.

Are you going to spend your whole life like that?

A sheepish smile is the answer.

멋쩍은 미소

성난 눈빛
의심의 눈초리
애원하는 눈길
창살 밖 어디를 어슬렁거리나

아무리 크게 눈을 뜨고
뚫어지게 바라보아도
어둠 가운데 잡히는 건 없다
간절한 상상만이
신호를 날려 깊이를 재본다
공을 건네 봐도 반응이 없다
받는 이가 있는 건지
어딘가로 사라졌는지
받고서 때를 가늠하는지
대답을 못 얻은 질문이
세상엔 얼마나 많은가

받을 걸로 알고 계속
신호를 보내는 거겠지
평생을 그렇게 지나려는가
멋쩍은 미소가 대답이다

Victor

Does the victor really

take it all alone?

Who is the winner?

What is all?

If the winner isn't really a winner,

he won't have anything.

If all is not really all,

there will be no 'winner-take-all'.

Who decides the winner by what?

By whom and how is the share determined?

If the winner is truly a winner,

the winner will know that all is not all.

승자

승자는 실로
혼자 다 차지하는 건가

누가 승자인가
무엇이 다인가

승자가 진정 승자가 아니면
아무것도 못 가지게 되리

다가 진정 다가 아니면
승자독식은 없게 되리

누가 무엇으로 승자를 정하나
뭇은 누가 어떻게 정하는 건가

승자가 진정 승자이면
다가 다가 아님을 알게 되리

Outerwear

A strong fire separated
him and his family.
Suddenly he was carried by a fiery whirlwind
and soared high and far into the sky*.

After a while, his figure
was not seen again,
and his outwear fallen off his body
was put into an urn.

His ashes reposed in an ossuary
alongside his wife who died three years ago.
It was the moment when the mission of this world
entrusted to them was completed with all sincerity.

The rain clouds were pushed away during the funeral
and the sky was high and blue and dazzling.
But that night**, a heavy rain and wind
blew through a thunderstorm.

* 2 Kings 2:11
** August 30, 2021

겉옷

강한 불길이 그와
가족 사이를 갈라놓는다
그는 홀연히 불 회오리바람에 실려
높이 멀리 하늘로 솟아오른다*

얼마 후 그의 모습은
다시 보이지 아니하고
그의 몸에서 떨어진 겉옷을
주섬주섬 단지에 담아 넣는다

그의 유해는 삼 년 전에 소천한
아내와 나란히 납골당에 안치된다
그들에게 맡겨진 이 세상의 임무가
빠짐없이 성심껏 완수되는 순간이다

장례 동안 비구름을 비집고
하늘은 높고 푸르고 눈부셨다
그러나 이날 밤** 천둥번개에
큰 비바람이 스쳐 갔다

* 열왕기 하 2:11
** 2021년 8월 30일

Park Road

It is a quiet park road
with no people or cars.
All the roads are left empty
for the farewell ceremony to pass.

The leaves are fluttering in various colors.
Which way do they want to enter?
When I ask if they're lonely and alienated,
They say, 'we don't have time
to be lonely to chase our ways.'

Most fall on the road or along the roadside,
some on the branches,
rarely rise up with the wind.
It's not easy even on earth,
but are they trying to find a way in heaven?

Who does hold up
those who stumble?
In what order
do the fallen get raised?

공원길

사람도 차도 없는
소음 없는 공원길이다
작별의 행사가 지나가게
길을 모두 비워두었다

갖은 색깔을 뽐내며
어지러이 날리는 잎들
어느 길로 접어들려나
소외되어 외로운가 물으니
갈길 쫓느라 겨를 없단다

대부분 길 위나 길가에
더러는 나뭇가지에 낙착한다
드물게는 바람 타고 솟아오른다
땅에서도 쉽지 않은데
하늘에서 길을 찾으려는가

비틀거리는 자들은
누가 붙들어 세워주는지
쓰러진 자들은
어떤 순서로 일으켜주는지

Things You Don't Even Know

A white butterfly is swaying in the wind.
What are you going to do here alone?
Do you think time is right for you?

Where are all the others
and you are wandering alone?
Are you a scout or a straggler?

Hiding behind a tree to avoid the wind,
it looked back and forth
and flew to somewhere.

This butterfly must have come this far
after going through many transformations.
It must be gasping not to miss the next turn.

For things you don't even know,
you are to run on a road you don't even know,
until the time you don't even know.

알다가도 모를 일

흰나비가 바람에 휘둘린다
어느 때인데 홀로 나와
여기서 무얼 하려는가

다른 이들은 다 어디 가고
너만 홀로 떠도는가
너는 척후병인가 도망자인가

바람을 피해 나무 뒤에 숨어
이리저리 무언 갈 돌아보더니
헐레벌떡 어딘가로 날아간다

많은 탈바꿈을 지나서야
여기까지 오게 되었으리
다음 차례를 안 놓치려 헐떡이지

너는 알다가도 모를 일로
알다가도 모를 길을
알다가도 모를 때까지 달려가게 되리

As It Leans

As the soul is drawn,
the mind is leaning.
As the mind turns,
the body follows.

The world is dragged, leaned and turned around.
Earth is drawn to the sun and turns around it,
and electrons are attracted to protons and rotate.
The galaxy is dragged by the universe and spins around.

You, too, are drawn to something,
and are following it somewhere.
I'm also attracted to somewhere,
and I'm chasing someone now.

쏠리는 대로

영혼이 끌리는 대로
마음은 쏠리고
마음이 도는 대로
몸이 따라가지

세상은 끌리고 쏠려 돌아가지
지구는 태양에 끌려 돌고
전자는 양자에 쏠려 돌지
은하는 우주에 끌려 따라가지

너도 무엇엔가 쏠려서
어딘가로 그걸 따라가고 있지
나도 어딘가에 끌려서
지금 누군가를 쫓아가고 있지

The Winding River

Along the winding river
Our yearning flows.
How faraway is the road we have to follow!
We are to cross the horizon ceaselessly.
In the boundless field where
Our longing is waiting for,
A wistful mood like a mist
Covers over the remote mountain.

Riding on the undulating waves
Our love runs on.
How distant is the ocean we should cross!
We climbs over the sea line endlessly.
Our waiting sings a song
Of the burning horizon.
Longing will open incessantly
The endless sea of hope.

(From "The River Unstoppable")

굽이치는 강물

굽이치는 강물 따라
우리의 동경은 흐르고
아득하다 가야 할 길
한없이 지평을 넘네
그리움이 기다리는
가없는 벌판에서
아쉬움은 아지랑이처럼
먼 산 너머로 서려가지

요동치는 파도를 타고
우리의 사랑은 흐르고
아련하다 건너야 할 바다
하염없이 수평을 넘네
기다림이 불러주는
놀 타는 지평의 노래
그리움은 희망의 문
끊임없이 바다를 열어가리

(“멈출 수 없는 강물” 중에서)

저자 약력

Lee Won-Ro

Poet as well as medical doctor (cardiologist), professor, chancellor of hospitals and university president, Lee Won-Ro`s career has been prominent in his brilliant literary activities along with his extensive experiences and contributions in medical science and practice.

Lee Won-Ro is the author of forty-four poetry books along with eleven anthologies. He also published extensively including ten books related to medicine both for professionals and general readership.

Lee Won-Ro`s poetic world pursues the universal themes with profound aesthetic enthusiasm. His work combines wisdom and knowledge derived from his scientific background with his artistic power stemming from creative imagination and astute intuition. Lee Won-Ro`s verse embroiders refined tints and serene tones on the fabric of embellished words. Poet Lee Won-Ro explores the universe in conjunction with his expertise in intellectual, affective and spiritual domains as a specialist in medicine and science to create his unique artistic world.

This book along with "Revival", "The Promise", "Time Capsule", "The Tea

Cup and the Sea", " The Tunnel of Waves", "Tomorrow Within Today", "Our Home", "The Sound of the Wind", "Flowers and Stars", "Red Berries", "Dialogue", "Corona Panic", "Chorus", "Waves", "Thanks and Empathy", "A Mural of Sounds", "Focal Point", "Day Break", "Prelude to a Pigrimage", "Rehearsal", "TimeLapse Panorama", "Eve Celebration", "A Trumpet Call", "Right on Cue", "Why Do You Push My Back", "Space Walk", "Phoenix Parade", "The Vortex of Dances", "Pearling", "Priming Water", "A Glint of Light", "The River Unstoppable", "Song of Stars", "The Land of Floral Buds", "A Flute Player", "The Glow of a Firefly", "Resonance", "Wrinkles in Time", "Wedding Day", "Synapse". "Miracles are Everywhere", "Unity in Variety" and "Signal Hunter" are available at Amazon.com/author/leewonro or kdp.amazon.com/book shelf(paperbacks and e-books).

글쓴이

이원로

시인이자 의사(심장전문의), 교수, 명예의료원장, 전대학교총장인 이원로 시인은 『월간문학』으로 등단, 『빛과 소리를 넘어서』 『햇빛 유난한 날에』 『청진기와 망원경』 『팬터마임』 『피아니시모』 『모자이크』 『순간의 창』 『바람의 지도』 『우주의 배꼽』 『시집가는 날』 『시냅스』 『기적은 어디에나』 『화이부동』 『신호추적자』 『시간의 주름』 『울림』 『반딧불』 『피리 부는 사람』 『꽃눈 나라』 『별들의 노래』 『멈출 수 없는 강물』 『섬광』 『마중물』 『진주 잡이』 『춤의 소용돌이』 『우주유영』 『어찌 등을 미시나요』 『불사조 행렬』 『마침 좋은 때에』 『나팔소리』 『전야제』 『타임랩스 파노라마』 『장도의 서막』 『새벽』 『초점』 『소리 벽화』 『물결』 『감사와 공감』 『합창』 『코로나 공황』 『대화』 『빨간 열매』 『꽃과 별』 『바람 소리』 『우리 집』 『오늘 안의 내일』 『파도의 터널』 『찻잔과 바다』 『타임 캡슐』 『약속』 『소생』 등 44권의 시집과 11권의 시선집을 출간했다. 시집 외에도 그는 전공분야의 교과서와 의학정보를 일반인들에게 쉽게 전달하기 위한 실용서를 여러 권 집필했다.

이원로 시인의 시 세계에는 생명의 근원적 주제에 대한 탐색이 담겨져 있다. 그의 작품은 과학과 의학에서 유래된 지혜와 지식을 배경으로 기민한 통찰력과 상상력을 동원하여 진실하고 아름답고 영원한 우주를 추구하고 있다. 그의 시는 순화된 색조와 우아한 운율의 언어로 예술적 동경을 수놓아간다. 이원로 시인은 과학과 의학전문가로서의 지성적, 감성적, 영적 경험을 바탕으로 그의 독특한 예술 세계를 개척해가고 있다.

이 시집을 비롯하여 『소생』 『약속』 『타임캡슐』 『찻잔과 바다』『파도의 터널』 『오늘 안의 내일』 『우리집』 『바람 소리』 『꽃과 별』 『빨간 열매』 『대화』 『코로나 공황』 『합창』 『물결』 『감사와 공감』 『소리 벽화』 『초점』 『새벽』 『장도의 서막』 『타임랩스 파노라마』 『전야제』 『나팔소리』『마침 좋은 때에』 『어찌 등을 미시나요』 『우주유영』 『불사조 행렬』 『춤의 소용돌이』 『진주잡이』 『마중물』 『섬광』 『멈출 수 없는 강물』 『별들의 노래』 『꽃눈 나라』 『피리 부는 사람』 『반딧불』 『울림』 『시집가는 날』 『시냅스』 『기적은 어디에나』 『화이부동』 『신호추적자』 『시간의 주름』 등은 아래에서 구입할 수 있다.

Amazon.com/author/leewonro와

kdp.amazon.com/bookshelf(paperbacks and e-books)

이원로 11번째 시선집

나의 강

초판 인쇄 · 2022년 11월 10일

초판 발행 · 2022년 11월 15일

지은이 · 이원로

펴낸이 · 이선희

펴낸곳 · 한국문연

서울 서대문구 증가로 31길 39, 202호

출판등록 1988년 3월 3일 제3-188호

대표전화 302-2717 | 팩스 · 6442-6053

디지털 현대시 www.koreapoem.co.kr

이메일 koreapoem@hanmail.net

ISBN 978-89-6104-325-0 03810

값 15,000원